ACT YOUR AGE SHAWN TRENELL!

By Breanya C·Hogue

Illustrated by Jasmine Mills

D1708146

ISBN-13: 978-1717551863
ISBN-10: 1717551866

Published by:
Breanya Hogue
sankofaky@gmail.com

Illustrated by Jasmine Mills

Dedicated to the rambunctious Shawn Trenells everywhere
and their patient educators and guardians.

Shawn was getting to "that" age. He was ten years old and about to head to middle school the very next school year. Everyone around him kept suggesting that he begin to "act his age." He was trying his very best, but was having a very difficult time...

Just that morning he jumped out of bed...literally, as his mom walked into his room to wake him up for school. He jumped down from the top bunk and landed his body in a perfect cannon ball on his toys below. His toy skateboard went soaring like a bird toward his mother's forehead.

BANG!

She looked pretty mad, but instead of yelling, exhaled, "Could you please act your age Shawn Trenell?"

On the bus, he tried his very best to behave. During the ride he decided he'd chew on his new double bubble, blueberry-raspberry flavored chewing gum while listening to his music.

He chewed and he chewed. Finally, he blew a bubble as big as a globe! Before anyone could see this grand sight, the bubble popped and some landed on the seat, the window, and his seatmate's hair!

Li Jing screeched and ran to get the bus monitor, who proceeded back to the seat, handed Shawn a bus referral, and this time did yell, "Could you please act your age Shawn Trenell?"

In the library, Ms. Greno chose Shawn to be her "special helper of the day." This was so exciting for Shawn, as teachers hardly ever chose him to be the class helper. He was so determined to do his very best job!

"You get to help me put all the books away back on these..."

RIIINNNGGG!!!

"One second, don't touch anything, I'll be right back," she explained, just as the library telephone rang.

Shawn sat...and he sat...and he decided to get a head start on putting the books away. He figured he would do a good job and show Ms. Greno how he could be the best helper ever... better than Alisa Fent (the class' teacher pet and most behaved student in the school). To reach the top shelf, he decided to make a ladder out of some of the books. He proceeded to construct a tall ladder and began to climb. When he got about midway, the books below began to wobble like he was balancing on jello. He tried to freeze, but it was too late...

BOOM!

The books made a loud **BOOM**, crashing down, all around. All of the students in the library began laughing and applauding. Ms. Greno ran back in an instant! Trying to avoid any more ruckus in the library and with anger in her tone she whispered sternly, "Could you please act your age Shawn Trenell?" She pointed him back towards his table to have a seat. With a frown and his head hung low, Shawn moped back, passing Alisa Fent, who was pointing and laughing.

Later in the day, during guidance class, the counselor, Mr. Trents began his lesson.

"Today we are going to talk about growing up. It is time for everyone to start maturing and acting their age."

"Act my age? Act my age? Act my age? This sounds familiar!" Shawn thought to himself.

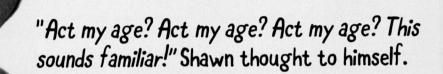

Shawn's hand shot into the air, "But, Mr. Trents, how can I ACT my age? I really, really, REALLY want to do it!"

Mr. Trents smiled at Shawn. He heard about the incidents Shawn had on the bus and in school that day. He responded, "Great question Shawn. You're still a kid and its okay to have fun, but be careful and pay close attention to your actions and how they affect others around you."

During the bus ride home, Shawn thought about all the mistakes he made that day and everything Mr. Trents taught him.

Later that night, when he got home, he practiced "acting his age" by being "responsible" and cleaning his room.

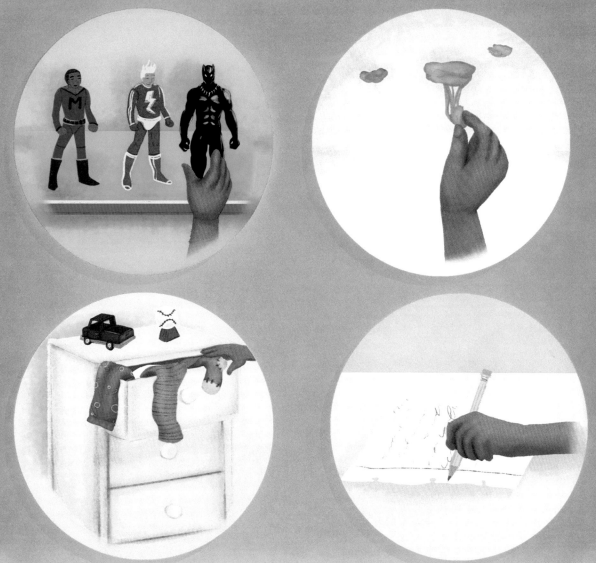

He organized his hundreds of action figures neatly, according to their super powers. He scrubbed all of the double bubble gum off of the ceiling (from where he had slung shot them over the months). He placed the mountains of clothes scattered all on his floor in their appropriate drawers, and last but not least, he decided to get started on his homework instead of catching up on the latest episode of "Captain Underpants."

In the other room, Shawn's mom was becoming worried because she hadn't heard any explosions coming from his room...as she normally did.

She decided to go and check on him. When she opened his door she was amazed. "Well, look what we have here!" she said with a smile, "Wow, you sure are..."

Cutting off her next words, Shawn interjected, excitedly, "I'm acting my age??"

At that very moment Shawn's mom realized that maybe she had been pushing him to "grow up" a little too much. After all, he was only ten. His mom laughed, "Shawn, I know momma has been telling you to "act your age" lately, but actually you have been doing just that. What I've really been meaning to say is to be thoughtful, mindful, and careful. I love you and I'm so proud of you. How about we go to the park and grab us some ice cream?"

Shawn could barely contain himself. He was about to launch across the room, charging into his mom with excitement, when he caught himself, remembering his mom's and Mr. Trent's words. He instead paused and exhaled, "Ah mom, that sounds like a great idea!"

ABOUT THE AUTHOR

BREANYA CHARISE HOGUE possesses a passion for writing which was shaped by experiences from her childhood, her career as an educator and as an advocate for CDF Freedom Schools Program. She earned both her Master of Education in School Counseling (K-12) and a Bachelor of Science in Early Elementary Education (K-5), with a concentration in English as a Second Language from the University of Louisville. Her love for community enrichment as well as student academic and family support pushed her to start providing her own services, through Sankofa-KY, which provides education consulting, mentoring, tutoring, staff training and more to partners. Breanya is currently pursuing her doctorate in Literacy, Culture, and Language Education at Indiana University and instructs literacy methods and teacher inquiry courses to undergraduate pre-service teachers. She enjoys traveling, meeting new people, helping others, and event planning. Lastly, she is a proud member of Delta Sigma Theta Sorority, Incorporated.

89683648R00015

Made in the USA
Lexington, KY
01 June 2018